I Am Really A Princess

by Carol Diggory Shields

illustrated by Paul Meisel

A PUFFIN UNICORN

For Richard, who is really a prince CDS

For Cheryl PM

PUFFIN UNICORN BOOKS
Published by the Penguin Group
Penguin Books USA Inc., 375 Hudson Street, New York, New York 10014, U.S.A.
Penguin Books Ltd, 27 Wrights Lane, London W8 5TZ, England
Penguin Books Australia Ltd, Ringwood, Victoria, Australia
Penguin Books Canada Ltd, 10 Alcorn Avenue, Toronto, Ontario, Canada M4V 3B2
Penguin Books (N.Z.) Ltd, 182-190 Wairau Road, Auckland 10, New Zealand
Penguin Books Ltd, Registered Offices: Harmondsworth, Middlesex, England
Text copyright © 1993 by Carol Diggory Shields
Illustrations copyright © 1993 by Paul Meisel
All rights reserved.
Unicorn is a registered trademark of Dutton Children's Books,
a division of Penguin Books USA Inc.
Library of Congress number 91-37161
ISBN 0-14-055857-8
Published in the United States by Dutton Children's Books,
a division of Penguin Books USA Inc.
Designer: Amy Berniker
Printed in Hong Kong
First Puffin Unicorn Edition 1996
1 3 5 7 9 10 8 6 4 2

I AM REALLY A PRINCESS is also available in hardcover from Dutton Children's Books.

I am really a princess.

And when my true parents, the king and queen, find out how
I've been treated around here, they are going to be very upset.

"No!" the king will cry. "Pick up your clothes and set the table? Scrub the tub and feed the fish and cheer up the baby? Do they think you are a servant? Everyday chores are not for a princess— a princess has far more important things to do."

"Like riding her pony, rescuing princes,

and dancing before her mirror in scarves."

"What?" The queen will frown. "They won't let you have a pony? But every princess needs a pony. A silver-footed, shiny-coated, prancing, dancing, just-right-for-a-princess pony. Of course he can sleep in your room."

"Share a room with that girl they call your sister?" the king and
queen will gasp. "Never! You are our only darling daughter, and
your very own room is waiting. Tower-high, with a balcony, a bouncy
bed soft as a cloud, shelves of books, toys, paints, and puzzles, and
behind the shelves, a secret passage, known only to you."

"It is a shame," their Highnesses will agree, "that they let you have only one lonely goldfish for a pet. A princess needs a noble dog who does clever tricks, a calico kitten to cuddle and chase.

"She needs a red-and-green parrot she's teaching to talk, a silky-skinned snake to curl round her waist."

"Lessons?" the queen will snort. "Piano lessons? Don't they know that a princess doesn't need to be taught? A true princess tosses back her hair and plays up and down, up and down the keys with both hands. Delicate trills and crashing crescendos, music so lovely all will cheer when you're done."

"No friends sleeping over, except on the weekends?" the queen will laugh. "That's a silly old rule! Here in the castle your friends are most welcome, anytime, night or day. Build tents out of blankets, stay up all night talking, play chess or checkers, have big pillow fights!"

"Quiet?" the king will bellow. "They expect a princess to be quiet? A really real princess roars like a lion, chatters like a monkey, and howls like a wolf!

"A princess should whistle and yodel and shout as loud as she wants. Babies in our kingdom *like* a lot of noise when they're sleeping."

"Punished?" they will sob. "Punished for digging those holes in the yard? Don't they know that you must have a moat round your castle, a moat deep and wide, with a drawbridge across?

"Don't they know that a princess must have tunnels, long secret tunnels, to quickly escape? Don't they know that tunnels are more important than tulips?"

"Help?" the queen will sniff. "A princess needs no help to dress. A princess does it all by herself and always looks divine. I like your superhero shirt with your ballerina skirt, polka-dot tights, purple cape, and red cowboy boots. And your bicycle helmet, of course. Perfect."

"Subtracting?" they will weep. "Not more subtracting! But you already did subtracting once! Surely a princess should be learning new subjects, like planets, or dinosaurs, or how to speak Chinese."

"Lima beans!" They will shudder. "Lima beans? But a princess never eats anything mushy. Any food you dislike will be banned from the kingdom. Pizza for breakfast? Peach pie before dinner? The royal chef waits for your command."

"Bedtime," the queen will say very sadly. "Bedtime so early? You mean you have to get ready for bed when *they* say so?

"But a princess goes to bed when she pleases. A princess needs time to gaze at the moon, to make good-night wishes on every bright star, to lie cozy and warm in her pillows and quilts, reading a book in the glow of her flashlight. Except when she chooses to sleep late on some mornings, a princess actually needs very little sleep."

"Tickle?" Their Highnesses would be shocked. "Tickle a princess? Tickle and tease you, cuddle and squeeze you? Do they think they can snuggle and hug a princess as if she were some ordinary child? Are you going to allow this type of behavior?"

Well...maybe just this once.

But one of these days, this family will find out who I really am. And they are going to be very surprised.

Because I am really a princess.

◆　◆　◆